Bubba heard a whale

trying to sing

words by Bubba's Dad
illustrated by Faryn Hughes

Illustration by Faryn Hughes
Book design by Kurt Mueller

CreateSpace Independent Publishing Platform,
North Charleston, SC

ISBN-13: 978-1727163322
ISBN-10: 172716332X

Dedication

To my Grandma,
who loved me and was proud of
me, just the way I am.

Bubba

Chapter 1

Every winter when the snow started to pile up higher than Bubba's very big ears, Bubba and his mom and dad would pile into the Bubbaru wagon and drive all the way from Minnesota to California.

There was a place there on the big blue ocean that Bubba loved more than any other place in the world.

It was a magical place called the Dog Beach…

Where Bubba would do zoomies across the sand and through the surf…

With a Bubba lime green ball held firmly in his mouth…

For hours and hours…

And that's where Bubba was today…

With two of his best California friends, Figgy and Spanky.

"Bark, bark, bark…gimme the ball, gimme the ball, gimme the ball," Figgy barked over and over.

"Zoom, zoom, zoom…let's zoom, zoom, zoom!" barked Figgy's brother Spanky as he raced alongside, water flying everywhere.

Boston Terriers can run super-fast, so Figgy and Spanky had no problem keeping up with Bubba—even though Bubba was one of the fastest French Bulldogs ever born.

They may have been equally good at zoomies, but Figgy and Spanky were better barkers than Bubba. Probably because they got more practice.

Bubba wasn't much of a barker. He would sometimes go months without barking.

But when he was at the Dog Beach, things were different.

At the Dog Beach he was so excited and happy that sometimes he would stop zooming and drop the ball and bark, bark, bark right along with all the other happy, excited dogs.

"Bark, bark, bark!" Bubba happily barked.

"Bark, bark, bark!" Figgy and Spanky happily barked back.

But then amid all the barking, something strange happened.

Bubba suddenly stopped barking.

And tilted his head.

His very big Bubba ears heard something.

And his stubby Bubba tail stopped wagging and froze in place.

Bubba listened. Listened very carefully. With his very big ears.

Spanky looked at Bubba and stopped barking, too.

"What do you hear, Bubba?" asked Spanky.

Even Figgy stopped barking, which was something he rarely did.

"What do you hear, Bubba?" asked Figgy.

"Someone is sad," said Bubba.

"Who is it?" said Figgy.

"I don't know," said Bubba,
tilting his head the other
way, a perplexed look
on his face.

"It's ... it's coming from out there in the big blue ocean."

"Why are they sad?" asked Spanky, looking worried.

"I don't know," said Bubba.

"They just went silent."

Chapter 2

Bubba went back to the Dog Beach early the next morning.

It was so early that the fog was just starting to lift from the beach.

It was so early that there was only one other dog when Bubba got there.

Quincy was a Newfoundland.

And he was busy scanning the big blue ocean for signs of sailors in distress.

Quincy never actually had to save a sailor in distress.

But one time he did save a little green sand pail that drifted out to sea.

Bubba looked very small next to his big black furry friend.

"Hi, Quincy," said Bubba.

"Hi, Bubba," said Quincy, without taking his eyes off the big blue ocean.

The two friends sat quietly and looked out to sea together.

Bubba closed his eyes and listened, listened very carefully with his very big ears.

And that's when he heard it. Again.

That sad little voice.

Out in the big blue ocean.

Bubba locked on to the sound with his ears.

It wasn't just a voice. It was also a vibration...

And...

A song!

It was like someone trying to sing a song.

But couldn't get the words out.

Bubba looked up at his friend.

"Quincy, can you hear that?"

"Yes, I can," said Quincy without looking down.

"Someone needs help."

"Who is it?" asked Bubba. "Maybe I can help."

Quincy jumped to his feet.

"Out there, Bubba, look!"

Bubba and his big ears jumped up and followed Quincy's gaze.

Out in the big blue ocean, just beyond where the waves rose up and started to curl, Bubba saw something he had never seen before.

A spout of water shot into the air. And then another. And another.

And then, one after another, where the spouts of water had been, three little humpback whales jumped into the air and landed with a SPLASH!

Bubba listened. He could hear and feel the whales singing.

They all sounded so happy.

Happy to be whales.

Happy to have each other.

Happy to have a song to sing.

All of them but one.

"There Bubba," said Quincy.

"Off to the side. Can you see her?"

Bubba could see her. One little whale appeared and disappeared. Her little hump barely breaking the surface.

"Why is she swimming alone?" Bubba asked.

"I don't know, Bubba, but it's not safe to swim alone." said Quincy.

"Maybe you could talk to her?"

"With your ears, I mean."

"I will try," said Bubba.

"Good," said Quincy, looking down the beach.

"I know you will do your best."

Then Quincy headed off to keep an eye on two little kids who were playing in the sand with a little green pail near the edge of the big blue ocean.

Chapter 3

Bubba scanned the big blue ocean with his big Bubba ears.

When he found the sad little whale trying to sing...

He locked on to her coordinates.

And began transmitting lime green Bubba vibes in...3...2...1...

"Hello," said Bubba very gently, so as not to frighten the sad little whale.

The little humpback whale's flippers turned pink.

She wasn't alarmed by the Bubba vibes. Vibrations are how whales talk to each other.

But she wasn't used to anyone ever saying hi to her.

So, she turned her head to the side, closed her eyes, and felt her flippers become uncomfortably warm.

"Hello, my name is Bubba, what's your name?" the French Bulldog asked.

The little whale went to the surface to take an extra-long breath and then dove deep under the water.

Bubba waited...

And waited...

"Hello? Are you there?" he asked.

"Shy," the sad little whale answered at last.

"I'm Shy."

"I mean, that's my name. My mama calls me Shy."

"Because I am."

Bubba's stubby tail wagged.

"That's a cute name," said Bubba.

Shy's flippers got pink all over again. And she didn't know what to say.

After a really long time she said...

"I have to go."

After another really long pause she said...

"My mama says I have to go to choir practice."

Bubba thought that was kind of funny.

Whales sing so it makes sense that they would have choir practice.

But it was still kind of funny.

Bubba's stubby tail wagged again.

"Can I send you some more vibes tomorrow?" asked Bubba.

Bubba listened. And listened.

Hoping for an answer. But none came.

He thought
his ears might
have a bad connection...

Because he couldn't hear anything.

Until after a really long time...

He heard Shy's very shy voice say...

"Yes, I would like that."

Chapter 4

Bubba thought about his new whale friend as he walked back to the Bubba beach bungalow.

He wished that she wasn't sad.

He wished he knew how to help.

At the top of the path leading down to the beach was a quiet little park with lots of pretty flowers.

As he stepped into the little park, his Bubba ears heard a Frenchie humming softly to herself.

Bubba's stubby Bubba tail wagged at the sound.

"Hi, Ryder," Bubba said.

A cute Frenchie girl's head popped out from a patch of pink, white, orange and yellow flowers.

"Oh...hi, Bubba," she said.

"What are you doing?" asked Bubba.

"Picking flowers," said Ryder, going back to picking flowers.

There was a long pause.

"All by yourself?" asked Bubba.

"Yep," said Ryder.

Bubba waited for Ryder to say something else.

But she didn't say anything.

So Bubba said something.

"Ryder, are you shy?" asked Bubba.

Ryder stopped humming to herself and looked closely at the flowers in her paw.

"I guess so," she said.

Bubba thought for a moment.

"Ryder, am I shy?"

Ryder giggled and her ears turned pink.

"No, Bubba, you aren't shy."

They were quiet for a little longer and then Bubba had a thought.

"Ryder, does being shy ever make you sad?"

"Sometimes," said the cute Frenchie girl.

"What do you do then?" asked Bubba.

Ryder lifted some pink, white and yellow flowers over her Frenchie ears, closed her eyes, smiled a big Frenchie smile, and twirled around in a circle.

"I put a crown of flowers on my head and pretend I'm the Queen of the Flowers!"

"Does that help?" asked Bubba.

"Sometimes," said Ryder.

"Hmm," said Bubba.

Bubba thought some more.

"I just met someone who is very shy," he said.

"And very sad."

"What should I do?" asked Bubba.

Ryder handed Bubba a flower.

"Just be her friend, Bubba."

"That's all you have to do."

Bubba took the flower and wagged his stubby tail.

"Thank you, Ryder," Bubba said.

"You're welcome," said Ryder.

Then the shy Frenchie girl went back to humming to herself and picking flowers.

And the not-at-all-shy Bubba went back to thinking about how to help his new friend.

Chapter 5

Deep under the surface of the big blue ocean the little whales were having choir practice.

First, they sang their whale song together.

And then they sang it one by one.

It went like this:

We are humpback whales
We all sing this song
It's the one we sing
It's how we get along

The vibrations they made while they sang were quite lovely.

If you were another whale, or Bubba, you could actually hear the color of the vibrations.

They were blue and gray and a sparkly silver.

And they traveled for miles and miles under the water.

When the little whales finished singing, the bubbles and vibrations slowly faded away.

"Very good, class," said Miss Forte, the choir teacher.

Her vibrations were kind but firm.

The class listened closely when she spoke.

"That was very nice...
but there was something missing."

The little whales all looked at each other.

"Shy, why weren't you singing?" Miss Forte asked.

All eyes turned toward Bubba's new friend.

Shy's flippers turned bright pink.

Several of the little whales started whispering to each other.

Bubbles from their whispers floated to the surface.

Shy looked down at the ocean floor and wished with all her heart that she could become invisible.

Miss Forte cleared her throat and the bubble whispers stopped immediately.

She swam over to the shy little whale and looked at her with her kind eyes.

But when she spoke it was with her firm, confident teacher voice.

"Shy, our whale recital is next week."

"And you will be singing."

"Singing beautifully, I might add."

The teacher's confident vibrations washed over Shy.

And for a moment she thought maybe, just maybe she could do it.

But then the weight of the whole big blue ocean was pressing down on her again.

And she wished with all her heart she could disappear.

Chapter 6

Shy was helping her mama blow bubbles to make a bubble net to catch something for dinner when Bubba's vibrations came through.

The mama whale and the little whale both stopped blowing bubbles and listened.

Shy looked sheepishly at her mom.

Her mom looked surprised at first. But then she smiled and said,

"It's for you."

Shy's flippers turned pink.

"It is?" said Shy, knowing that it was.

"I'll let you take your call in private," her mom said.

Then she smiled again and slowly swam away.

Shy watched her go and waited until she was sure no one else could hear Bubba's vibes.

"Hello?" said the shy little whale.

"Hi, Shy, it's Bubba."

"Hi Bubba," said Shy, her vibrations brightening and her flippers getting even pinker.

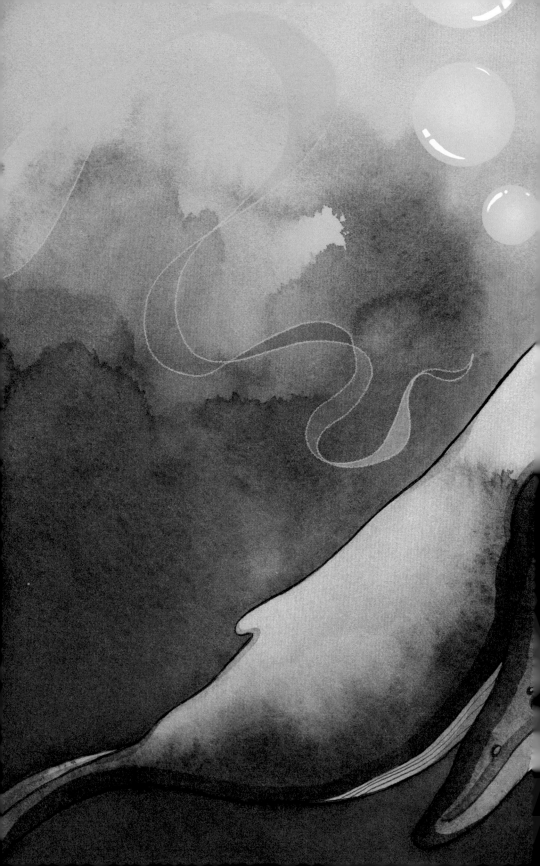

"How are you today?" asked her new Frenchie friend.

Shy's vibrations turned a sad color.

"Not so good."

"What's wrong?" asked Bubba.

"I have a choir recital next week."

"Don't you like to sing?" Bubba asked.

Shy paused for a really long time before answering.

"No, I don't like to sing," she said softly.

Bubba could feel the sadness in his little whale friend's vibes.

"How come?" asked Bubba gently.

The salty sea water turned a little saltier around Shy's eyes.

Bubba waited a moment and then asked his new friend a difficult question.

"Shy, why don't you sing like the other whales?"

Somehow, Shy knew she could trust Bubba, so she told him something she had never told anyone before.

"Because I'm different," she said.

"Their song isn't my song."

"And I don't feel right singing it."

The vibrations from the ocean stopped and Bubba could feel how lonely the little whale felt.

And it made him feel sad.

Bubba sighed a long Bubba sigh.

Then he tilted his head and thought a long Bubba thought.

And his stubby Bubba tail did a quick wag.

Bubba was thinking of another friend who was different.

And Bubba was pretty sure he could help.

Chapter 7

Bubba stopped by to see his friend Auggie on his way to the beach.

Auggie was on his porch watching a butterfly open and close its wings.

He didn't hear Bubba hop up on the porch behind him.

But he knew he was there because he could feel his Bubba footsteps on the wooden floor.

Bubba sat down next to his friend and watched the butterfly, too.

The butterfly's wings were dark on the outside and they burst into color each time they opened.

Auggie smiled and nudged Bubba with his shoulder and Bubba nudged him back.

Auggie was different than most Frenchies.

That's because he was a deaf Frenchie.

And while he couldn't hear sounds the way other Frenchies could, Auggie could see and feel things that other Frenchies sometimes missed.

Bubba was very good at doggy sign language, so he had no problem talking with Auggie...

Which was a good thing because
he learned a lot from his deaf friend.

"Auggie, do you ever feel different?"

"Sometimes," said Auggie.

"Does it make you sad?" asked Bubba.

"No, I kind of like it."

"It makes me proud to be different," said Auggie.

"Really?" said Bubba.

Auggie looked at Bubba with his kind, wise Auggie eyes.

"Really!" smiled Auggie.

"I have a friend who is different. And it makes her sad," said Bubba.

Auggie could see and feel the sadness in Bubba's eyes.

"Bubba, could you do me a favor?" Auggie asked his friend.

"Sure," said Bubba.

"Look at that butterfly. See how happy it looks when it spreads its wings?"

Bubba watched the butterfly open and close its wings.

Each time its wings opened he saw a little burst of color.

And with each burst of color Bubba wagged his stubby Bubba tail.

"It makes me feel happy, too," said Bubba.

"That's right, Bubba. It feels good when you let the true you shine through."

"Even if you're different?" asked Bubba.

"Especially if you're different," said Auggie.

The two Frenchies watched the colorful little butterfly in silence.

"I think I will tell my friend to let her true self shine through," said Bubba.

"That's a great idea," said Auggie.

After sitting quietly for a while, Bubba gently nudged his friend with his shoulder.

"Thanks, Auggie," said Bubba.

"You're welcome," Auggie smiled.

Chapter 8

Shy was trying to sing.

And it wasn't going too well.

Her vibrations were a pale blue and gray
that didn't look or sound quite like other whales.

And they didn't really look or sound like her own
either.

Just when she was about to burst into tears,
something nice happened.

Bubba's lime green vibes arrived from shore.

"Hi Shy, it's Bubba," said the little whale's Frenchie
friend.

"Hi Bubba," said Shy, blinking tears out of her eyes.

"How is choir practice coming along?" he asked.

"Not very well," she said.

"Can I help?" asked Bubba.

"Tell me what's wrong."

Shy sighed and a few sad bubbles bubbled up to
the surface.

"I just can't get the words out," she said.

Bubba thought for a moment about what his friend Auggie had told him.

"Do you think it would help if they were your own words?"

"What do you mean?" asked Shy.

"What if you sang your own song. One that let the true you shine through?"

Shy thought for a moment.

Her mood brightened and her vibrations started getting brighter, too.

"How would it go?" asked the shy little whale.

"Can you give me the words to sing?"

Bubba smiled on the other end of the lime green vibrations.

"Shy, it's your song. The words have to come from you," he said gently.

"Hmm, I guess they do," said Shy, thinking.

And that's when Bubba asked a very good, very helpful question.

"If you could sing any kind of song. A song that was yours and yours alone. What kind of song would that song be?"

Shy thought a really long time.

And then she thought some more.

Suddenly it came to her!

"It would be a soft, happy song."

"And it wouldn't be blue and gray like other whales."

"It would be pink and gold like I feel inside."

"And it would go like this..."

That's when Shy closed her eyes and started humming her song.

A few notes at a time.

As she hummed, her vibrations started to change color from blue and gray to pink and gold.

And they began to glow as she started to sing the words.

> *I'm a shy little whale*
> *This is my song*
> *It's soft and happy*
> *I hope you'll sing along*

When Shy stopped singing the soft pink and gold vibrations gently faded away.

And then she opened her eyes.

"What do you think?" she asked Bubba quietly.

"I think it's beautiful," Bubba said.

"It's the true you."

This made Shy very happy.

And then Bubba asked her a question that made her even happier.

"Shy, can I come to your recital?"

Shy's flippers turned pinker than pink.

At first, she didn't know what to say.

"You would do that?"

"For me?"

Bubba's stubby tail wagged faster than fast.

"Of course I will. I'm your friend."

Then his Bubba vibes glowed bright lime green and he said...

"I'll be there. I promise!"

Chapter 9

Bubba was waiting for Cherie the Surf Dog at the Dog Beach.

He was wearing his Bubba lime green life jacket and standing knee deep in the surf.

He didn't like to go in too deep by himself.

As the surf came in and out, it would wash up to his Bubba belly.

And that was deep enough.

Bubba looked out to sea when his very big ears heard a very big wave heading his way.

And that's when he saw her.

It was Cherie the surfing Frenchie!

Her surfboard was pink on top and green on the bottom.

And she rode the big wave like a champion surfer.

Because that's what she was.

Bubba knew this because he had seen her surfing trophies himself.

When Cherie saw Bubba she crouched down on the board and steered it all the way into shore.

"Hi, Cherie!" said Bubba.

Cherie smiled at her old friend.

"Ready to go whale watching, bro?" she asked in her cute California accent.

"You betcha," said Bubba in his cute Minnesota accent.

And with that, Bubba hopped on the pink surfboard and he and his surfer friend paddled out to sea.

Chapter 10

Bubba's very big ears locked on to the sound of the little whales warming up for their recital.

"Over there," he said to Cherie the Surf Dog.

And they both Frenchie-paddled the pink surfboard toward a calm spot on the big blue ocean.

Far below the surface, Miss Forte, the whale choir director, was preparing to start the show.

The little whales were all lined up in a row with their eyes on their teacher.

The littlest, shyest whale was on the end.

Her eyes were mostly on the teacher, too.

But occasionally she would glance nervously up at the surface...

Hoping Bubba would get there soon the way he promised.

She also looked out into the audience where her mom and the other whale parents smiled proudly.

Shy started to feel a sinking feeling.

Bubba had given her lots of confidence that she could sing her song.

But at that moment she wasn't so sure anymore.

Shy closed her eyes.

And listened.

Hoping he would come. He just had to, she thought.

And that's when she heard it.

She couldn't believe her sonar!

It was Bubba. And he was right above her!

Shy's flippers turned very, very pink and she blinked away tears of happiness when she felt Bubba's lime green vibes.

"Hi, Shy," said Bubba.

"You came!" Shy exclaimed.

"Of course I came," said Bubba, wagging his stubby Bubba tail.

"I saved you a seat," said Shy excitedly.

She quickly swam over to a raft of bubbles she and her mom blew earlier.

It was tied to a bed of seaweed and when Shy released it, the bubbles floated to the surface next to Cherie's surfboard.

Shy looked back at Miss Forte and quickly took her place in the choir.

She whispered to Bubba.

"The recital is about to begin! I'll give you a ride home when it's over."

"Thanks!" Bubba whispered back.

Then he hopped on the bubble raft
and made himself comfortable.

"Cherie, Shy's going to give me a ride back."

"I'll see you tomorrow, okay?"

"That would be awesome, dude. Enjoy the show!"
smiled Cherie.

As the surfing Frenchie caught the next wave back
to shore, the whale recital began.

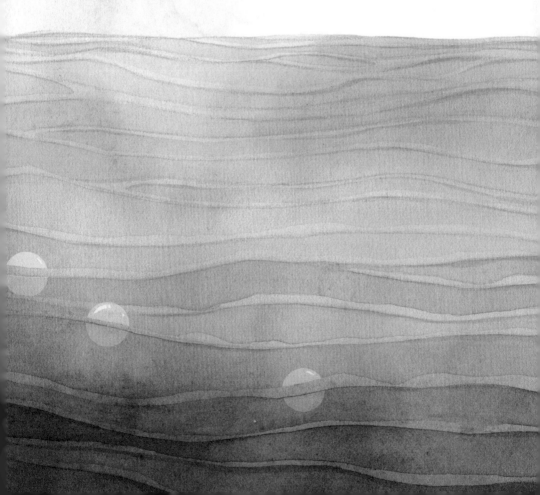

Miss Forte cleared her throat.

All the little whales paused and then began
to sing their whale song.

As they sang they also began to gracefully swim in
a circle...

Swimming in and out of their blue and gray and
sparkly silver vibrations.

First, they sang their song together.

> *We are humpback whales*
> *We all sing this song*
> *It's the one we sing*
> *It's how we get along*

Then they each did a solo with the solo singer taking
a spot in the middle of the circle.

It was quite lovely...

But with each solo, Shy became a little more shy and
nervous.

She could feel her confidence slipping away again.

Maybe if she quietly swam off no one would even miss
her, she thought.

But before she could slip away, she found herself in the middle of the circle.

Alone.

With everyone watching. And listening.

Shy closed her eyes tightly.

Suddenly, everything went quiet.

Miss Forte was waiting...

Shy's mama was waiting...

All the little whales were waiting...

And that's when she felt it.

A confident vibration that said...

"Sing your song."

"Let the true you shine through."

Shy wasn't sure if the confident vibration came from Bubba or from somewhere else.

But the moment she felt it all of her fears slipped away and she started to sing.

Very softly at first. And then more confidently.

I'm a shy little whale
This is my song
It's soft and happy
I hope you'll sing along

As she sang, the vibrations around her started to change color.

The blue and gray and silver turned to a beautiful pink and gold.

Everyone in the audience listened closely.

They had never heard a song like this before.

But the closer they listened, the more they liked it.

As the pink and gold vibrations grew brighter and warmer, the whole big blue ocean grew quiet.

For miles and miles, sea creatures big and small stopped to listen. And the song they heard made them feel happy.

Up on his bubble raft, Bubba's stubby tail was wagging faster than it ever wagged before.

His friend's true self was shining through. And it was beautiful.

Miss Forte thought it was beautiful, too.

She motioned to the rest of the choir...

And soon the whole little whale choir was singing in perfect harmony.

Chapter 11

After the recital ended, all the little whales told Shy how much they loved her song.

Even the ones who hadn't noticed her before.

And then Shy introduced them all to Bubba.

The other little whales had never met a French Bulldog before.

And they were kind of impressed that Shy knew one.

Then Shy gave Bubba a ride back to shore.

The little whale glided smoothly just under
the surface of the biggest wave she could find...

With Bubba surfing on the tip of her nose...

His big Bubba ears flapping in the wind...

And Shy happily spraying a happy spout of water.

As they came near the Dog Beach...

And Bubba got ready to hop off and Frenchie-paddle
to shore...

They both agreed this was the best day ever.

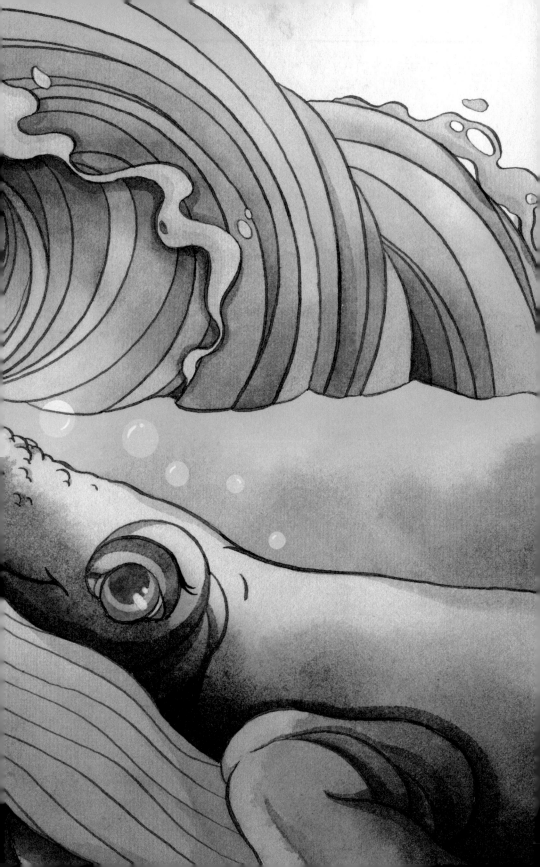

Chapter 11½

Every afternoon Bubba would go back to the Dog Beach.

After doing lots of zoomies, Bubba would curl up on the soft sand and close his eyes.

As he dozed off under the warm California sun, his Bubba ears wouldn't doze.

They would listen, listen very carefully...

To the sound of the waves gently lapping the shore...

And a beautiful little whale song...

Unlike any other song in the whole world.

It was his friend's song.

And it made his stubby Bubba tail very happy.

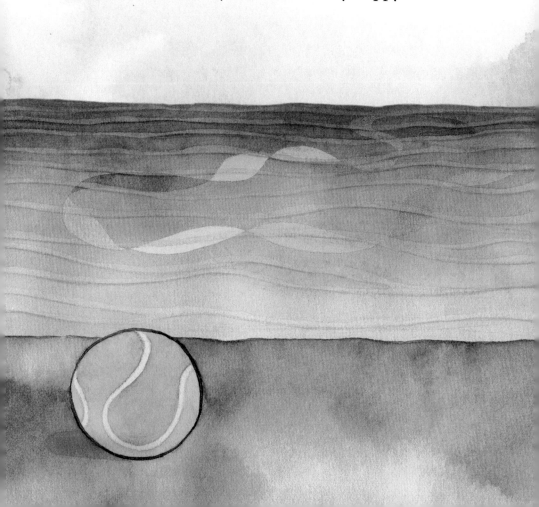

That is all.

Made in the USA
Middletown, DE
30 September 2018